BLOOMFIELD TOWNSHIP PUBLIC LIBRARY

W9-BVO-171

BLOOMFIELD TOWNSHIP PUBLIC LIBRARY
1099 Lone Pine Road
Bloomfield Hills, Michigan 48302-2410

A Story of Courage in the Mayan Tradition
The Bravest Flute

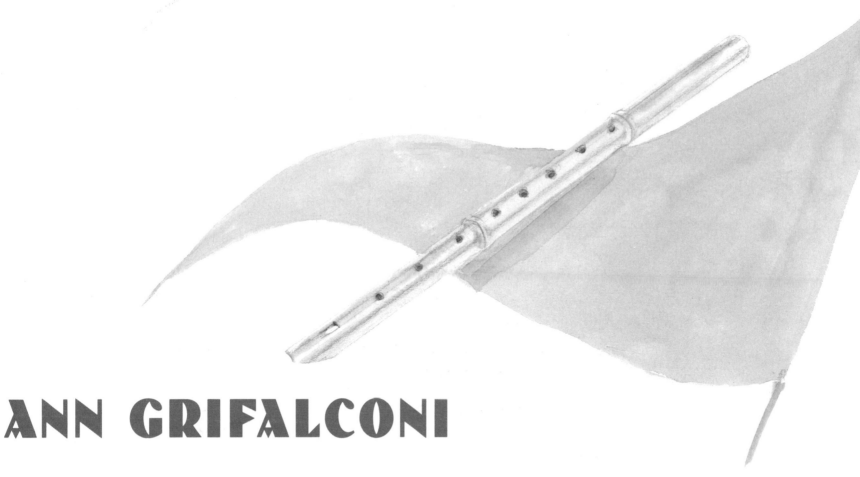

ANN GRIFALCONI

Little, Brown and Company

Boston   New York   Toronto   London

BLOOMFIELD TOWNSHIP PUBLIC LIBRARY
1099 Lone Pine Road
Bloomfield Hills, Michigan 48302-2410

Author's Note

The boy in this story is one of the Maya of Central America, the direct descendants of the mysterious ancient Maya. These were a people who had for thousands of years maintained a very high civilization based on corn cultivation, in the region of what is now Guatemala, Honduras, the Yucatán, and southern Mexico.

Today, at four million or more strong, the sturdy and artistic Maya remain one of the largest groups of Native Americans. A proud people, they struggle to retain and rebuild their heritage and faithfully continue to observe their spiritual and communal traditions.

The rural Maya of the highlands are mostly farmers, working under very difficult conditions of poor land and economic oppression. They use what land is left to them in order to raise their own food: corn, beans, and squash. Through a system of true cooperation between men, women, and children, these hardworking people try to balance their lives by continuing to practice their many arts such as music, poetry, pottery, and weaving.

Copyright © 1994 by Ann Grifalconi

All rights reserved. No part of this book may be reproduced in any form or by any electronic or mechanical means, including information storage and retrieval systems, without permission in writing from the publisher, except by a reviewer who may quote brief passages in a review.

First Edition

Library of Congress Cataloging-in-Publication Data

Grifalconi, Ann.
   The bravest flute : a story of courage in the Mayan tradition / Ann Grifalconi. — 1st ed.
      p.   cm.
   Summary: In a traditional New Year's Day celebration, a young Mayan boy leads a procession over the mountainous trail to the cathedral below, where he is rewarded by the village elders for his fortitude.
   ISBN 0-316-32878-2
   1. Mayas — Juvenile fiction. [1. Mayas — Fiction. 2. Indians of Mexico — Fiction. 3. Indians of Central America — Fiction. 4. New Year — Fiction.]
I. Title.
PZ7.G8813Br   1994
[E] — dc20   93-5217

10 9 8 7 6 5 4 3 2 1

NIL

Published simultaneously in Canada by Little, Brown & Company (Canada) Limited and in Great Britain by Little, Brown and Company (UK) Limited

Printed in Italy

Have you ever played a flute
Until the sound burst in your head?
Until your chest burned
Your lips bonded to the mouthpiece
That single entrance
For your song?

Yet bravely
Cutting through the thick, reluctant air
Arching over the dark night
Of all other causes
Lyric sound comes forth
Singing of that which is
Dreamed, fragile
Single
Threatened.

And slowly, after time
The reedy tone rises
And lifts a softness into the day
Sustains, note by note
A surprising steadiness
A surer purpose
Until other voices, awakened
Chant in answer!

JAN 27 1995 B & TAYLOR

The high, clear call of the cock startled the boy awake.
Though he had slept in his woolen poncho, he was shivering in the chilly mountain air.
Trying to ignore the cold and a fresh pang of hunger, the boy stretched out in a yawn,
And his fingers touched the smooth length of his bamboo flute.
He smiled. He would answer the cock's song with one of his own!
Then he sat up suddenly, remembering: *It is New Year's Day!*
The day he was to lead the parade to town, while playing his flute!
This was to be his first task of service to the community,
Bringing honor to him and his family!

Picking up his hat and his flute,
The boy moved silently past the warmth of the hearth,
Where his mother and sister still slept nearby.
Let them rest a little longer! he thought.
The family had been struggling so hard to stay alive farming the hard, rocky soil,
Hunger had even driven them to eat the seed corn to survive!
There was a covered clay pot resting on the banked embers,
But he knew it held only a little corn gruel, and he left it for them.
Cinching his belt tighter, the boy stepped out into the dawn.

Then the boy stood still for a moment,
Holding his hands under the front of his poncho against the cold,
Trying to catch sight of the morning star, Ixyoki, before it faded away.
It was said that Ixyoki was the messenger of hope,
And he needed a message of hope — and strength — right now!

For there was one great problem: not only must he play his flute,
He would also have to carry the great drum on his back, all day long!
The drummer, walking behind, would bang on it loudly with his sticks,
All the while calling the country folk to follow them to town.
Then he must lead them even up to the very steps of the cathedral,
Where the elders would be waiting to seat the leaders of the New Year!
And he must complete his task — all the way!
Ever since his father had died, he'd had to think of his family:
He knew that if this journey was bravely done, and with a song,
The elders might gift him with pesos — to buy seed corn for the coming year!

He saw the morning star begin to disappear behind the rising mists of day.

The boy looked over at the flickering star, his worries clouding his vision.
"Just one more minute!" he whispered,
Drawing the star's fading light into himself.
"If you last, then maybe I can, too."
Closing his eyes, beginning to fill with tired tears,
He thought, *If it is still there when I open them . . .*
By the time the boy opened his eyes,
The mists rising from the mountains all about
Had formed a huge rainbow-colored ring in the sky over his head!
Holding his breath in awe at this miraculous sight,
The boy saw that the morning star, also, still twinkled there
Like a diamond set in the great ring!
At such good omen, he set his hat upon his head, his flute to his lips
And took off down his path, playing his song.

Reaching the drummer's thatch-roofed house,
The boy saw the villagers had already gathered for the great day.
The women, bustling about like bright birds
In their embroidered cotton blouses and warm woolen skirts,
Were busy serving cups of good hot *atolé*,
The honey-sweetened drink of ground red corn saved for this day.
The men were making much of getting out the big drum,
Many proudly wearing colored head-scarves or wide-brimmed black hats —
Signs of honor and rank earned from their years of service to the community.

I, *too, may someday become one of these men of importance,*
Thought the boy as he hungrily held a clay cup to his lips,
If I last out this day of service! But first, I must make myself strong!
And he drank the hearty liquid down.
The drummer came out of his house then, in his magnificent outfit.
What a sight he made! Straightening his shoulders,
The boy walked over to the men clustered about the great drum —
The drum looking bigger and bigger the closer he got!

Seeing that the boy chosen to carry his fine drum was so small and weak,
The drummer nervously directed the men attaching the drum to its harness.
Feeling the sudden weight of the drum, the boy took a step, laughing out loud.
The drummer looked up in surprise.
"Now I know just how a turtle feels!" the boy exclaimed.
The men all laughed, too. "But this turtle has a voice!"
The boy answered bravely, "And this turtle has a song!"
And he began to play upon his flute as he stepped firmly forward.
The drummer saw that perhaps he had been wrong. This boy had spirit!
"If we stay in step," he said to the boy, "we will do well this day!"

The two stepped forth onto the footpath that would lead them over hill and dale
To the great town, so far away.
As the boy played upon his flute, the drummer ended each flight of song
With a great *thump!* that echoed far and wide.
The people came from their lonely mountain homes, gaily dressed,
Lining up behind them and trailing over the hills,
Following flute and drum.

And so they went, the drummer and the boy carrying the big drum.
And the beat of the drum rang like a gong inside the boy's head
As he tried to chase it out with the song of his flute.
And he staggered slowly down into the valleys, and up again,
And he knew he could not stop.

Near the last part of their journey, the rocky footpath joined the asphalt road.
Unsteady by now and tired, the boy worried because of the slick surface ahead.
He made his tired legs take one shaky step and then another, advancing slowly.
If he could only lift his head, maybe he could see the town,
See the cathedral towers rising high, built upon the pyramids of his ancestors.

But the boy had to keep his eyes on the road,
Playing his song forward, following it, one step after another...
Then above his song, he began to hear a growing rustle,
A rattle, voices calling — a swelling roar!

He was walking on soft leaves laid out on his path!
He was being pelted with flowers and paper streamers, and people were cheering!
He had entered the town itself!

He was passing through many arches made of green pines,
Lifting high overhead and all the way down the street before him!
And on either side, people waving, children laughing, dogs running...

The boy tries to lift his head as he walks,
Tries to blow his flute as the sweat pours down his face...
Only a few more steps...

Past the stern faces of the elders, robed in black and red . . .

Past the matrons of the Society of Weavers...

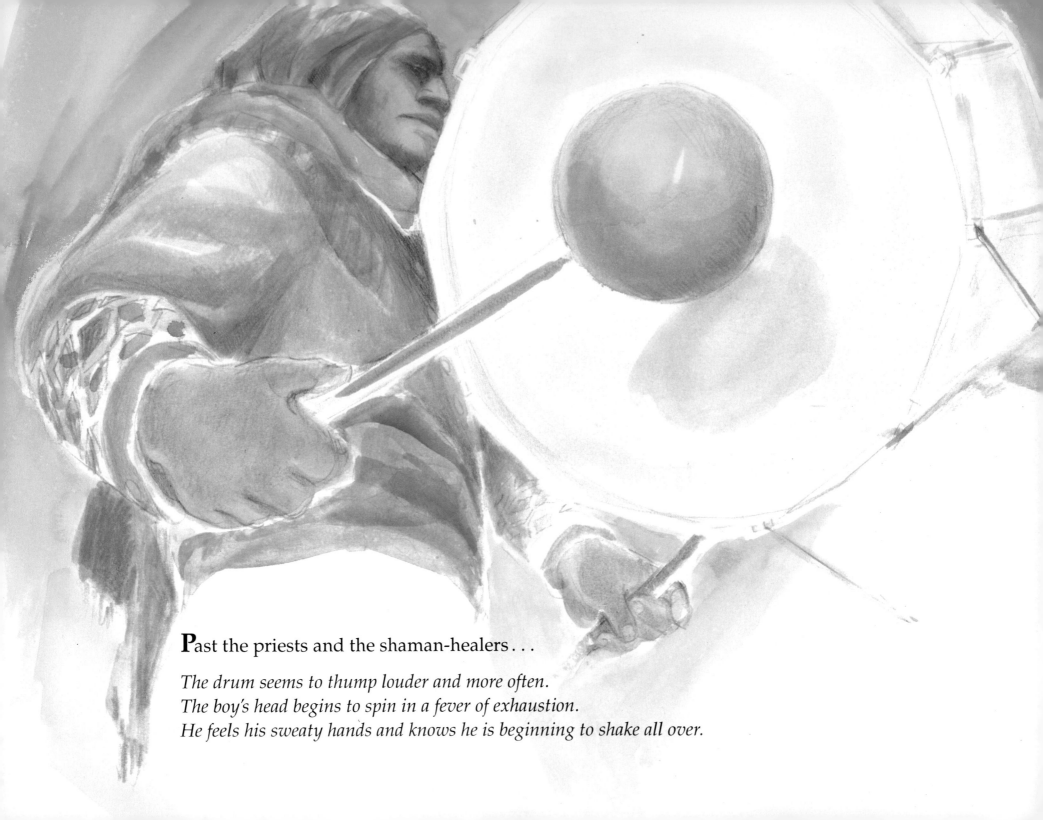

Past the priests and the shaman-healers...

The drum seems to thump louder and more often.
The boy's head begins to spin in a fever of exhaustion.
He feels his sweaty hands and knows he is beginning to shake all over.

Can he make it to the end of town — to the cathedral itself?

His throat tightens.
His breath begins to fail.
Can he still blow his flute?

The flute in his hands
Begins to waver in front of him
Like a reed in a high wind.

A woman with a kind face — who looks somehow familiar —
Leans toward him, gives him a sip of water from a flask.
Then something flashes as she puts it in his hand!

*All of a sudden everything has become white!
He thinks he has stepped into a cloud.*

Every step he takes seems easy, light, effortless,
And the weight of the drum on his back is somehow lifted.
And the flute? It feels different!

Still half in a daze, the boy looked at his flute.
It had turned into a master flute, all black and silver, in his hands!
There was the silver mouthpiece, set into the carved length of black wood.
But how . . . why? The kind-faced woman! *This* was what had flashed in her hand!
Then he remembered: she was the widow of the old master flutist.
She must have given him her husband's flute!

Cautiously, the boy began to blow into it.
And the sweetest music he had ever heard came out of it,
Spiraling all about him!
Was it because of the magic sound that he felt new strength flow into him?
For more and more firmly his songs went out,
And more and more boldly the boy stepped forward,
Sending messages of joy before him.

Flags flew by, and smiling faces.
Then the boy saw the cathedral steps rising ahead of him!

The elders, with their staffs of office, were waiting for him on the topmost step.
A few steps more . . .
He had made the journey of his life this day!

Now the boy kneels with the elders on the topmost step,
His head bared in prayer.
He holds his hat, now red-ribboned, in one hand,
In the other, the brave new flute!

And in his shoulder bag he carried the five round coins
The elders had awarded him ("For you have earned it!" they had said)
To buy food for his family
And seed
For the year to come.